THE ARRANGEMENT

Vol. 9

H.M. Ward

www.SexyAwesomeBooks.com

Laree Bailey Press

COPYRIGHT

Laree Bailey Press
First Edition: July 2013
ISBN 978-0615859767

THE ARRANGEMENT

Vol. 9

CHAPTER 1

After blinking several times, as if my eyes are broken, my brain finally catches up with the situation. My gaze narrows while I step towards Marty with malice in my eyes. Too many emotions clash together too fast. I can't fathom what he's done, what it means. My hands want to ball up into fists and find his face for ruining the fragile relationship we had left. I need him, and he goes and does something like this. Marty's friendship is important to me and the guy's flushed it away like a goddamn goldfish.

Add to that the issues I'm having with Miss Black and my mind shorts out. There's a big spray of mental sparks before my vision turns red.

Marty's confident expression washes away. The smug smile on his face is gone as he steps back, holding up his hands—palms toward me—in a classic don't-kill-me pose. "Avery, wait a second—"

"How could you?" I jam my finger into his chest as I advance. The door clicks shut behind me after I step into the room.

Marty's voice is nearly shrill. It has that freaked out airy sound that people have when they're about to get a stiletto shoved up their ass. "I didn't! It's not what you think. Give me a chance—"

"I already gave you another chance. I already did this with you! You couldn't just leave it alone! You couldn't just—" An aggravated sound tears from the back of my throat as my palms slam down on his chest as hard as possible. My hands go flying, smacking and punching, without thought. I hate that he did this. I hate his stupid stringy tie and dumbass cowboy hat. I rip the hat off his head and throw it to the ground before snatching the bolo from his neck.

"Avery! Listen to me!" He has that nervous laugh he gets when something goes horribly wrong. Pleading, he smiles at me, and tries to explain. "You see, there were things, and none of them worked, so I—"

I'm not listening. I swear to God that I try. More than anything, I want this to make sense, but Marty buying me for a night and pretending to be the cowboy client makes me think he had plans to ride me all night. My jaw feels like it's going to pop out of place, because the muscle is way too tense.

There are moments that make sense when they happen, and it makes perfect sense to me now. I have to punch a card with Black so she doesn't skin my ass and hang it on her wall, and I have to manage to sleep with a guy—who I thought was my best friend. It's not a problem. Of course not. "You want me so bad you'd buy me? Well, fine." I laugh like I belong in a mental institution. My smile is too bright and my voice is too high. Arms spread wide, I say, "Here I am."

Marty blinks at me. When he opens his mouth again, I don't want to hear what he wants to say. I advance on him, tugging at his shirt, and ripping the front open. My foot stomps on his hat as I tear the shirt off his body. My foot crushes the felt and Marty stands there appalled.

"I think you have the wrong idea. Hey!" He tries to keep his shirt, but I grab hold of it and tug. Marty is talking, but it sounds like buzzing. This can't be my life. It can't be. There are so many things that I'd thought I'd be, so many things I thought I'd do, but none of them included screwing my best friend for cash. I jab, punch, and shove him as I rip his shirt off and toss it to the floor. I hurt so much. Sobs bubble up from my throat in an incoherent rage. "Avery, stop! This isn't what you think! You're too upset to see it now, but—" He tries to grab my shoulders, but I twist away.

"You don't know what you've done! Do you know what she'll do to me if I walk out of here right now? I can't do this, but I have to." Tears glitter in my eyes as I start laughing again. I can't think. I know what I have to do even though I don't want to.

What else is new? I've been living a life that I've hated for the past few years. What's another day?

It doesn't matter. It doesn't matter. It doesn't matter. I can fuck him and leave. That's what he wants. That's what he paid for. Do it and leave. The words repeat over and over again, drowning out everything, including Marty's girly screams and bitchslaps.

Marty is bare-chested, standing in front of me in jeans and boots. His hair is a mess and his eyes flash with fear. He sucks in a jagged breath and works his jaw as his fingers flex at his sides. "This isn't what you think. If you'd stop—"

I laugh, but it feels like someone drove a lance through the center of my chest. I want to fall face down on the bed and cry until I pass out, but I can't. There's no one left to pick up the pieces and I sure as hell won't let Marty see me fall apart. Looking crazy is fine, but turning into a ball of slobbering snot will never happen.

I snatch at his belt buckle, doing everything in my power to force myself forward. The god-ugly thing is a big piece of brass with a bird on it that connects to a black leather belt. I have to do this, I have no choice. He left me no choice... I'm snapping like a piece of balsa wood. I can't even form sentences any more. I'm saying things to him, half crying, slapping him and hugging him.

I can't... I can't... I can't...

Pain flashes in his eyes, as he continues to try and talk to me, but his mouth moves and there are no words. My eyes twitch, flicking around the room, on his face and at the door. Gabe is out there, watching, waiting. They're going to make sure I do it this time. I saw what was done to Henry. I can't take a beating like that. I'll end up with broken ribs and more medical bills that I can't afford.

Every muscle in my body is tense, ready to snap. I want to beat my fists into Marty and scream until I feel better, but nothing will fix this—nothing will make it better. He's gone too far this time. There's no way to recover from this, so I'm not showing a shred of mercy. It's me or Marty, and I'm not going to be the loser again. The past few times he pulled shit like this, I let it roll. The man pretended to be gay and went lingerie shopping with me. I didn't drive his jewels into his skull with my knee then, but I should have—and God knows he deserved it.

I tried so hard, so fucking hard, to make things better with him. I spilled my guts and let him get close to me, closer than I should have, and all the time I was thinking that this guy cares about me and wants my friendship, he was just trying to get laid. Fury shines through me like a beacon in the night. I can't control it. I can't calm down and I don't want to. Betrayal looks horrible on me.

"Avery, stop." He shrieks, as my nails catch the skin on his chest, and he dances away from me. "I'm so sorry, so sorry I did it this way. I shouldn't have. I know that now. I had no idea you were this far gone—"

He says things, his voice soft and coaxing, but they wash over me. I'm stuck in my head, trying my best to live through another horrible day, forcing up walls wherever I can so I can look at myself in the mirror tomorrow. When I reach for his belt this time, I manage to get the buckle open.

Marty stands there, stunned, with his mouth hanging open, and his eyes go blank like he can't believe this is really happening. The heavy metal buckle flicks open and falls to the side. When I reach for the button to his jeans, he snaps out of it. Marty's hands fly to my wrists. He shoves me away, but I won't stop. I have to finish. I have to do this.

White spots blink like stars in my field of vision as I reach for his waistband again and the room tips sideways. I stumble and blink a few times as a flood of heat hits me hard. It courses through my veins, from my toes to my eyelashes like an inferno.

Instead of swatting me away this time, Marty's hand darts out and takes hold of my wrist, pulling it high above my head. The motion forces me to stop. My feet are nearly off the ground when he tilts his chin down and breathes in my face. His voice is shaking, and comes out in a register so low that I can feel the force behind each staccato word. "For once in your goddamn life let someone else help you."

I laugh in his face and swing my other fist at his head, and miss. It'd be comical if I wasn't half crazed at the moment. "No! Stop lying to me! I can't take it anymore!" I swing at him again.

Marty effortlessly dodges my fist and I growl in response. My nails are biting into my palms as I plan another swing at his jaw. Marty grits his teeth and hisses at me, "I'm trying to help you. If I'd known you'd go batshit crazy, I would have had Mel here. She's going to kick my ass when she finds out that I broke you."

I laugh like I'm ready to mentally crack and take another swing at him. He grabs my fist with his other hand, and pulls me into a bear hug. I can't move. Tremors burst from inside of me and shake my body, "I can't do this. I can't…" I'm sobbing.

He holds me tight and continues to explain. "I know, sweetie. I know how upset you've been. I hired you to give you a break and keep you away from assholes like Henry Thomas. After what happened last weekend, I wanted to buy you some time, so that's what I did. I bought you tonight. I was trying to help."

Tilting my head up, I stare at him. Marty releases me and steps away with his back to me and runs his hands through his hair. He's strong. The muscles are tense beneath his skin, like he's going to lose it. He steps forward without warning, and slams his knuckles into the wall. The plaster cracks like frozen ice and his fist disappears behind the wallboard.

Marty pulls his fist from the wall and doesn't look at me. He sits down on the side of the bed with his back to me and lowers his head into his hands.

There's a long silence and I don't know what to do. I smooth my dress and take a seat by the little desk in the corner and try to calm down. I don't know what to do. "Miss Black—" I start to say something but can't finish. It feels like someone pulled my head off and screwed it back on, but failed to connect my mind. It's still wandering through a field of haze laced with complete and total despair. I hold my face in my hands and say, "What was I supposed to think, Marty? After everything that happened, what was I—"

There's a knock on the door that cuts me off. We both glance at it. Marty pads over and looks through the peephole before opening it. A young guy, wearing a hotel uniform, is standing there with a tray. "Your dinner, sir, and the movie you requested."

Marty nods and points to the desk where I'm sitting. The guy smiles at me and places the tray down. There are two silver domes covering hot food that smells like heaven, along with a movie—my favorite movie—*The Last Unicorn*.

A lump hardens in my throat as I stare at the DVD. My eyes burn, but I don't blink. I can't. I was so wrong, so horribly wrong. Marty didn't pick up a phone and order this stuff after I got here. He planned it before I came. Everything slams into me and it's like I'm getting pelted with bricks that won't stop. By the time Marty signs for the bill and sends the guy away, tears are streaking down my cheeks and my hands are trembling.

I try not to look up, but I have to. When our gazes lock, the only words that want to come from my lips are, "I'm sorry."

Marty nods, as his eyes cut to the side, landing on the movie on the tray. "I thought we'd eat and do stuff you like. I wanted to give you a break from all this, so you didn't have to think about anything for a while."

"Marty—"

"No, don't even try to say anything, because there's nothing you can say." He grabs his coat from the closet and heads toward the door, but he has to pass me to get out. "I should go. I'll send Mel over or something."

I stand quickly, blocking his way. "Look me in the eye and tell me that you didn't hope something sexual would happen. If it's the truth, tell me." My eyes are glassy when I look up into his face. The plea in my voice is clear enough—I don't want to lose him.

Marty's gaze meets mine and holds for half a beat before he shakes his head and looks away. "Intentions and hopes are two different things, but after this, you don't have to worry about either anymore." He tries to shoulder past me, but I step in front of him again.

"Don't leave things like this."

"Why would I stay? Look at you. I tried to make you happy and let you rest, and look what I've done. I'm not the right person. I messed it up. I thought you'd—"

his voice drifts off as his eyes lower. "I'm so sorry, Avery. I'd never do that to you— force you like that."

Marty steps past me and takes the knob in his hand. He stops and tenses before twisting the metal. My heartbeat jumps to stroke territory. Gabe is going to see him leave and not come back. It'll be another unfulfilled contract, and Black already threatened me. But, that isn't why I'm afraid. My pulse is pounding because I've made a horrible mistake, and I know if he walks out that door, I'll never see him again.

Marty is paused, stuck in place. It feels like hours, but it can't be more than a few seconds. I'm afraid of saying something, but saying nothing sounds like a bad idea, too. I start talking and have no idea where I'm going with it. "I remember when I first met you, how you were larger than life. You were always there, and it didn't matter what I'd done—you stood by me. We could have been good friends, maybe more, but it's too late now. The stupid part is one day I know I'll remember you and this won't be what comes to mind first. It'll be your decade style clothes and the way you said things so absurdly that I couldn't help but smile, or the way you seemed to show up at the right time, every time. When I remember you—"

His shoulders stiffen as I talk, like I'm stabbing him in the back over and over again. Then he rounds on me suddenly, and looks down into my face. His hands slip up my wet cheeks, wiping the tears away, as his gaze dips to my lips. Suddenly, he's there, kissing me and pressing his lips lightly to mine.

The emotional whiplash leaves me stunned, so I don't move. His lips press against mine, softly before deepening. The kiss doesn't last very long, but time has lost all measure. I keep thinking his lips are on mine and it's not disgusting. They feel nice, safe, and certain. Marty knows what he wants, and he wants to protect me. He loves me, without a doubt, I feel it coursing through him, especially when he pulls away and I see his eyes.

Stunned, I remain still and watch him turn to leave. "Good-bye, Avery." Just as he opens the door, I grab his wrist.

"Wait." My voice catches in my throat as I squeeze his arm harder. "Tell me how to fix it, because I can't let you leave."

His eyes drink me in like he'll never see me again. "I think I messed things up beyond that point, Avery."

"Nothing is ever past that point. Things only fall apart when one of us gives up, and it won't be me."

"It is with us. Besides, it only takes one person to end a relationship and I think I managed to mess this one up beyond repair." He presses his lips together, like he knows he's going to regret it. I feel him mentally leaving me behind and walking through the door without looking back.

Desperation fills my chest, I want him to stay, I want to fix this, but I don't know how. "Thank you." He glances at me, not understanding. "For the reprieve. I need it." A sad smile lines my lips, and nearly cracks my face into shards.

"So, why didn't you tell me?" Marty watches me closely, waiting for his meaning to show up on my face. Those dark eyes hold mine, and I know what he means— what he wants me to say.

My eyes fall to the side as my stomach twists. He knows how he makes me feel. I tuck my hair behind my ear and glance up at him. "I didn't know what it was." The feelings I have for him could be attraction or a myriad of anything else. It's hard to say. We've been through so much and everything got out of hand. "Don't go. I can't stand the idea of losing anyone else. Not tonight. Please, Marty. You were right. I need this. Stay with me?"

He smiles and looks up at my face. He sighs and then finally says, "At my apartment, after I picked you up at your parent's house that night... Things were weird between us the next morning. I felt it, and I know you did, too." He watches me, waiting for me to deny it.

"I don't know what that was, and I was such a wreck that night. It's hard to know what I felt."

Looking down at me with a vulnerable expression, he suggests, "Then let's settle it. One night, sleep next to me for one night—actual sleep—nothing else. If you feel anything for me, you'll know. It'll be like that night at my place, and you'll be certain."

The thought terrifies me. Is it possible that I like this guy and never noticed? Is that why we fight so much? Is that why I can't let him walk away? I let Sean walk away and I regret it horribly.

No more regrets. "All right, one night."

CHAPTER 2

The phrase, *This is weird*, keeps replaying through my head like a witch's chant. Marty is asleep next to me and it's the middle of the night. The clock on the nightstand blinks as another minute passes and the number changes. My heart is racing, like I'm scared about something. I wish I knew what it was. So much stuff has happened that it feels like I'm standing in the center of a vortex, getting my freakin' brains sucked out. I'm pretty sure they're all gone, because why am I here? Better yet, why does it offend me to sleep—literally sleep—with Marty, but I'm okay with sleeping with a stranger?

Stuffing the pillow under my head, I try to get comfortable, but I can't. I'm a liar. I lie to myself and everyone I know. My life has been torn to shreds and I'm the one who did it. Before Black, I was dirt poor— as in dirt for dinner was too expensive—but now friendships are too expensive. I've lost everyone who matters. Since the time I walked in on Sean and Mel, things with her have been weird, then Marty's confession threw me for a loop, and now Sean is gone.

I'm alone. It hits me like a boulder crashing down from space. I guess that's an asteroid, right? Oh God, it's so late and I'm so tired, but sleep won't come.

I roll the other way and see Marty's peaceful face. The first thing I think is, *He's not Sean*, and that's the problem. I like Marty, I can admit that. That little tug at the center of my chest when I see him is attraction. I'm not brain dead, it's just that someone else overshadows that little flirtation and Marty is eclipsed. Completely.

So, in the morning when I wake up, I can tell him that I like him—that he was right—but nothing good will come from it. Sometimes knowledge isn't freeing and those words will just trap him. Marty won't move on if I say those things. Lying to his face is going to suck, but I have to do it. Regret lines my mouth and tastes as awesome as burnt coffee grinds. I sucked this up. Maybe we both did.

My mind wanders to Mel and her advice to chase down Sean and propose. She's so insane. Well, it's not that the idea is insane, it's more that it's emotional suicide. If he said no, I think I'd walk right up to the top of the Empire State Building and throw myself off. Okay, that's too dramatic, but I'm so fried. After he says no, then what?

What if he doesn't say no? a little voice chirps inside my mind. *What if he says yes?*

And that's the issue—what if? The 'what ifs' suck. They wedge themselves into the corners of my mind and fuck up my life. What if I proposed? What if he said yes? What if we were happy and had two fat babies, a dog, and a little house with a white picket fence? What if I got everything I ever wanted? What if I wasn't a coward lying in bed next to a guy that I'm attracted to, but not in love with? Where would I be?

The reality of that answer makes me close my eyes and roll onto my back. Draping my arm over my face, I breathe in and out. If I wasn't with Marty right now, I'd be with a stranger. I'd be a hollow shell of a woman, selling my body so I don't have to eat freeze-dried noodles every night. It's not that simple, but in some ways it is. Grabbing a pillow, I pull it over my face and hold it there so I'm in a vice of fluffiness.

"Do you always try to suffocate yourself while you sleep?"

I toss the pillow on the floor and turn my head toward him. My eyes aren't filled with sleep like his. They're strained, tense, and tired. Words are bursting inside my mind and I haven't said a single thought out loud for hours. I have a plan. Lie to him, trick Black into thinking we did it, and hope I don't get my ass kicked when she finds out I'm lying.

Sighing, I fiddle with the black bead on my bracelet. "Nah, normally I try to jump out the window, but these are bolted shut."

He gives me a concerned look. "Kidding, Marty. I wouldn't be wrapped up in this crap with Black if I didn't want to survive."

"So, you're going to keep doing that?" He's on his side looking at me.

My eyes are downturned as my fingers play with the blankets. "I don't know... It pays well enough. Hey, I have a rude question for you—how'd you afford all this? I mean, Black isn't cheap, and requesting a specific girl jacks up the price."

He gives me a crooked smile. "I have some money—correction, I had some money, and credit cards. I used the rest of my student loans for the semester too. I'm going to write this off as an education expense and take a tax deduction."

I chuckle a little. "An educational experience?"

"Sure, why not. I think I learned more about human nature tonight than I did the entire time I've been in college."

"And what's that?"

"Don't buy friends that are hookers—they don't like it."

I smack him with my other pillow, before tucking it back under my head. "Hooking and friendship doesn't mix."

"Hooking and pancakes don't mix either. I'm never going to have the same thoughts about iHOP ever again, thanks to Mel."

That gets another light laugh, and my tired brain launches words out of my mouth. Before I have a second to think, I blurt it out. Maybe I suck, or maybe I don't—I don't know anymore. I just want to do something right and not make things messier, but I have a feeling that I should shut my mouth. Nothing good ever comes after 2am, and it's nearly an hour and a half later. "I don't want to lie anymore—not to you—and not to me. The truth is, I think you're great, but my brain didn't realize how great because you were under the gay guise—the mask of Gay-o."

"Was that a Zorro reference?"

"I don't know what it was, but the truth is I hate how messed up things are between us. I hate that I lost you. I hate that I like you. I hate that you're not who I thought you were, because there's some affection between us. I know it's there…" Marty's lips get this soft dreamy smile, which makes me feel horrible. Oh God, I shouldn't have said anything. Plowing through, I finish, "But—"

The grin vanishes. "Ah, the but…"

"But it's overshadowed by someone else. Marty, I—"

"You don't need to say more. I get it." He rolls onto his back and takes a deep breath, like I just kicked him in the 'nads.

I feel horrible, not better. Confession is good for the soul, my ass. "What would you have me do? Should we fake date? Should you be my rebound guy? Should we wing it and see what happens? Those are crappy choices, because in every single one of them, you're second. You don't deserve to be the runner-up, Marty. You deserve better than me."

"There is no one better than you."

"Then we're both screwed, because I suck." I nudge his elbow with mine, but he doesn't return the gesture. "Tell me what you want."

"I want you to get Sean out of your system. Either be with him or forget about him. This in the middle shit is driving me insane. I swear to God, being friends with you is beyond exhausting."

"I know, and I'm sorry." Sighing, I drape my arm over my eyes and say, "So, what are we? Is friendship off the table?"

He pushes up onto one elbow, lifts my wrist, and looks me in the eye. "What kind of an asshole do you think I am? Oh wait, don't answer that." He smiles down at me. "Yeah, we can be friends, maybe even friends that kiss?"

Laughing softly, I shake my head. "No kissing."

Marty considers it, like he's bargaining with some old lady at the flea market. "Okay, okay. I'll settle for friends with benefits." He winks at me.

"The only benefits you'll be getting are rides in my awesome car."

"Is that a euphemism?"

I laugh. "For what?"

"I have no idea. Your car sucks monkeys, like literally. It must have plowed down an entire gaggle of the hairy little suckers at some point. I mean, the smell alone..." I shove his arm and he laughs.

Running his hands over his face, he groans, "Oh God, Avery. It's like we both signed up to be miserable. You don't like me enough to do anything about it, and Sean ditched you."

I nod slowly, like something should become clear, and hope that a big fat unicorn will jump out of a rainbow that formed in the dark clouds that hang over my head. "We deserve a unicorn."

"I know what you mean, and I'm not even gay."

"You're brain damaged, like me."

"Fucking unicorns." He glances at me and we both start laughing. It's that sleepy giggly laugh that is difficult to stop. When we do, we're both on our own pillows, staring up at the ceiling. "So, are you going to make yourself more miserable, like me?"

"Probably, but I need you to be more specific."

"Are you going after him?"

I'm quiet for a moment, even though I already know the answer. Saying out loud that I'm going after Sean makes it real, admitting it to someone sets the concept in stone. I'm stepping into a pair of cement shoes and jumping off a bridge, willingly.

"Yeah, I have to see this through. I'll get down on one knee, hold up a ring, and shut my mouth until he answers me." I laugh, "You know, I don't think I can take any more stress. It feels like my life is held together with cobweb string. If things don't go well, I don't know how I'll get over it."

"Mel and me are here, Avery. We always will be, and if I ever run into Henry Thomas on the street, he better run the other way. Ditto for Mel. She described what she'd do to that bastard and it's not pretty. That woman is scary."

CHAPTER 3

Isolation is a weird thing. I'm not sure how it happened. It kind of snuck up on me after I lost my parents. My childhood friends faded to acquaintances and then fell into the shadows of my past. I have no desire to bring them back, either. People that are only there during the good times suck. I've had enough leeches in my life, and I'm grateful for the friends I have now. It hasn't escaped my notice that the people that I like the most are the kind that have been beaten by this life and didn't lie down, face first, in the dust. We gravitate toward one another. Maybe no one has an ordinary life, but since that's what I'm striving for, I'd rather not think about it. Chasing something that doesn't exist would completely suck.

I can imagine bringing Mel home to meet my Mom. First off, no one ever forgets meeting Mel. She's all personality in a mocha-skinned body with killer curves. It's hard not to notice how striking she is when the woman is standing in front of you. I think Mom would have liked her. Mel fights for what she wants and encourages me to do the same.

Right now we're standing in a jewelry store and I have a goofy smile on my face with bags under my eyes.

"He better appreciate this shit." Mel is crouched over a ring case, her eyes scanning diamonds, gold, and platinum for something that has an antique feel.

"I should probably just get a plain band. He's going to say no anyway."

Her gaze flicks up and her caramel eyes give me the you-crazy once over. "What are you going to do if he says yes?" She folds her arms across her chest and leans her hip into the case.

I start to open my mouth when a sales girl walks over. She's wearing a perfectly pale pink suit and is cute as a button. Mel's going to eat her—uh, like a lion, not a hooker. Perky chick says, "My name is Tiffany and I—"

Mel tilts her head to the side like she's annoyed and doesn't even look at the woman. "Listen, Stepford Psycho, we aren't going to take any crap, or hard sales, or whatever you have planned up there in your little plastic head, so walk away and if we find something to buy, I'll snap my fingers and you will pounce over like a good little bitch because you work on commission."

The sales girl's face falls, her mouth gaping open in horror. She's momentarily stunned, so Mel snaps her fingers. "Hear that?" The girl nods. "Good, now go over there until I call you. Go on. Scat. That's a good girl."

Tiffany's super pink pouty lips repress a sneer as she walks away. I glance at Mel. "Do you have to be so mean?"

"She's a bitch. Fake people deserve to be treated like they're made of tin—or plastic. I recycle, it's okay. Besides, you know how I feel about robots." She cringes and shakes her head. The expression on her face is reminiscent of the second before a woman realizes there's a spider crawling across her lips and into her mouth.

Strumming my fingers across the top of the glass case, I say, "Yes, I know you hate robots—"

"The fuckers are everywhere. If there's going to be an apocalypse, it's going to be from that bitch inside my phone—"

My fingers press to my temples and stare at her. "Oh my God, Mel. Not now. And I don't think the sales girl deserved to be verbally castrated because she likes pink."

Mel glances up at Tiffany. "Nah, I did it because she interrupted me. What was I saying?"

"What if he says yes…"

Mel nods, which makes her thick gold hoops sway back and forth. She seems to have an endless supply of huge-ass earrings. "Yeah, about that—you don't want him to have an ugly-ass ring for the rest of your life, do you?"

"No, but none of these are quite right." I glance over at her. Every scenario I can picture fades to black before I can even get the words out of my mouth. It's like the black hole of horror. My mind stops there and can't see beyond it. "Why do you think he'll say yes?"

"Because he thinks with his dick and we're gonna make it commandeer his brain."

I smirk at her. "Seriously, Mel. I need to know why."

She gives me a long hard look and exhales. "Because of the way he acted before he left. Something about it screamed overprotective, which could mean he's an asshole that planned on ruling your life, or he actually loves you. Since, he let you keep working for Black and skipped town, I'm guessing it's the latter. The boy may be scary as hell, but deep down he's a coward. He wouldn't have run off if he didn't care about you. Besides, that whole theory lines up with what his brother told you. Sean Ferro has the hots for you."

Her words are what I want to hear. No, they're better than that. They give me hope and I can't hide the stupid look that crosses my face. "So, what do I say?"

"You tackle him to the ground like a linebacker and shove the ring over his cock. Then you say, marry me. Easy peasy." Mel sees something in the case and snaps her fingers over and over again until Tiffany bounces over. Mel and Tiff exchange deadly smiles. Mel points to a ring. "I'd like to see that one."

Tiffany has one of those I'm-better-than-you-smiles on her face. "I'm sorry, but we only take jewelry out of the case for customers who intend to make a purchase."

Oh shit. I glance at Mel, almost afraid to see how she took it. Mel's face is perfectly smooth with the prettiest smile I've ever seen. She's at DEFCON 1 and ready to nuke the place. Just as Mel opens her mouth, I grab her arm and cut her off, "I'm hungry. Let's go to Friendly's and then keep shopping. And you—" I glare at the idiot sales girl. "I just saved your life. Remember to kiss my ass the next time you see me."

I pull Mel out of the store before she goes into a full rant. By the time she's onto heavy nostril breathing and death ray vision, we're seated at a little table. The truth is Friendly's is one of my favorite places to eat because my parents took me here when I was a kid. It was the special place that I could choose to go to whenever something awesome happened. Basically, it's a small diner that sells sundaes and milkshakes.

Mel's nostrils flare and she slams her hands on the table. "I'm going back there. She can't talk to me like that!"

"So, show her that she's a dumbass on the way out."

Mel smashes her lips together and grunts, "I will."

"Good." I open the menu even though I already know what I want. My eyes skim over the plastic pages, avoiding Mel's freaky pissed off gaze.

"I mean it." Her jaw is locked tight.

Laughing, I say, "I know."

I order for both of us and eat in silence as Mel stews across from me. She dabs a fry in ketchup over and over again with a vacant look in her eye. It's not a good look for her. It means she's thinking, no, plotting, and nothing good ever comes from that.

After a little bit, Mel stuffs her face as fast as she can and then taps her fingers on the tabletop while she waits for me to finish my sundae. It has peanut butter sauce and fudge, which means that I'm not hurrying.

"Oh. My. God. Hurry up, Avery. You're killing me."

I lick the fudge off the back of my spoon without thinking. The nerves that have been twisting my stomach into knots are finally fading. I think I might be able to find Sean and ask him without puking on him. Screw wine, chocolate does wonders for the nerves. "Done." I put my spoon down and Mel bounces out of her seat.

"I'll pay my half to you after you find me. See you in a second, okay?"

"Mel, where are you going?"

She flashes a wicked smile my way. "Back to the jewelry store, where else?" Before I can tell her that an assault charge will interfere with her life, she's gone.

I sit in the booth for a second and my phone chirps. I pull it out of my purse and thumb the screen to life. There's a text message from a number that I don't recognize. The area code isn't from around here.

Hey...

I type back, *Who's this?*

Someone who misses you.

My stomach swirls as I type in his name. *Sean?*

Yeah, baby. Do you miss me?

What I type doesn't convey how much. *Yes.*

I miss you too... I grin like a dork for a few seconds until his next message appears. *So, what are you earring?* Pause. I blink at the screen trying to figure that one out when it chimes again. *Ducking autocorrect.*

That makes me laugh. *Ikr? Damn dicks...* And I press send before I see the typo. I swear, smart phones were made to make people look stupid. *Ducks, ducks! I* type quickly and hit send.

Lol. Sure. There's a pause and then he sends, *I need to see you again.*

My heart rate picks up and thumps along at a million miles per hour as it soars through the sky. He wants to see me! I try to play it cool and decide to refrain from writing back *YYYYYEEEEEEESSSSS!!!!!* like an orgasmic hornball. I'm beaming. It's a sure thing now. If Sean can't leave me behind, he must want to be with me. My decision to ask him to marry me seems like a better plan now. I can't wait to see him, and I don't want to wait. I'm getting a ring and finding him tonight.

I type back, *I'd like that.*

Then I'll see you soon. I need to take care of a few things and then I'll be in touch.

Acid couldn't wipe the smile off my face after reading that.

When I finish at the restaurant, I pay the tab and then wander through the mall with a goofy look on my face, resisting the urge to skip and tap my heels together. Oh hell, I do it anyway. I skip twice, which is really more of a gallop, before I jump. When I go to tap my heels together, I miss. It's the most uncoordinated thing I've ever done. I come down with my ankle at a strange angle and fall on my ass.

A couple of guys clap loudly and chide, "Nice, honey! Way to stick the landing!" They laugh and walk by me like I'm too stupid to be alive, but I so don't care.

I jump up and brush off my butt with a huge blush across my face, giggling. The other guy winks at me, like I'm really cute. Who knew my super sucky coordination skills were attractive? I duck my head and scurry away before I manage to trip on my feet.

When I catch up to Mel in the jewelry store, Tiffany is glowering in the corner with her arms folded over her plastic boobs. I bounce up next to Mel. "What are you doing?"

She beams at me. "I figured I needed some stuff while we were here—ya know, some gold hoops, a 3 carat diamond pendant to match. Nothing much. My friend Roger here is ringing me up and I'm going to pay in cash." Her voice is so loud. If pride had a face, it would be Mel's. She beams at me as she lays out over $10,000 in cash, slapping it down on the counter, bill by bill, grinning.

Tiffany rolls her eyes. I wave her over and she looks hopeful. "Hey," I ask, "you got a second?" She nods, hoping that I'm going to spend as much as Mel. Like I'd spend it with her after that? Seriously, someone sniffed too many markers. We both glance at Mel. After a moment, I say, "It's too bad you went super bitch on her ass, before. On the bright side, you just pushed your friend's sales quota over the top for the month."

I beam at her and walk over to Mel, who's wearing her new jewelry. "Damn, that's a big diamond." It's a princess cut and looks stunning against her dark skin. The chain is white gold and matches the crusted diamond earrings she bought to match it.

Mel flashes her bright smile my way, actually giddy. "I know. I said to myself that I needed to buy myself a present. I work hard and I deserve nice shit, so I came back in here and Roger—this wonderful man— helped me pick out the biggest diamond pendant they had. Now it's mine!" She squeals and claps her hands together like she's too excited to breathe. Then, she looks over at Tiffany and waves. "Have a nice day, Bitchy Barbie."

CHAPTER 4

On the way home that afternoon, I get a call from Black. When I answer the phone, her voice is terse and the epitome of unfriendly. "Where are you?"

"I'm with Mel, why? Is something wrong?" What could go wrong at an illegal brothel? For a second I think the cops are raiding her office, but it's too quiet.

Black's teeth click together when she speaks. "You have a client this evening,

Avery. You need to stop in here before you go. It's late, so I reiterate—where are you?"

I'd planned on driving to Jersey tonight to find Sean. Mel glances at me out of the corner of her eye while driving Southern State like a race car driver. She cuts off a pickup truck who blares his horn at us. We're going to get caught in rush hour if we don't get back to the dorm soon. I need to pack a bag before I go.

"I didn't sign up to work tonight. Mel and I are off."

"You and Mel are both working. There are clients, Avery and—"

Pulling the phone away from my mouth, I whisper to Mel, "Are you working tonight?" She shakes her head. "Turns out we are. Can she do that?" Mel wiggles her fingers, meaning for me to give her the phone. "You can't drive and talk—" Mel snatches the phone from me. "Okay, so maybe you can…"

Mel's voice is as hard as Black's. "Hey, Miss Black. I was out with my home-fry, Avery. What up?" Mel mouths, "I'll handle this. No reason to go whiter than you already are. We need to get you some color, girl." Mel jerks the car and changes lanes, leaving my stomach behind us. I hate driving with her in traffic. She bobs and weaves, yanking the steering wheel, changing lanes abruptly, and flying like the car should have wings.

Mel grins, "Well, it's gonna cost you. We had plans." Mel presses the phone to her shoulder and cuts across three lanes of traffic to get to our exit. Horns blare, but somehow she still hears what Miss Black says. "Fine, whatever. All I know is that my days off are getting to be fewer and fewer, and overworked and underpaid are two words that are not in my vocabulary, Miss Black. So, if you want me and Avery to work tonight, you're going to have to fix that underpaid part. Overtime is a 50% increase. We're both well into it this month and you know it. Uh huh. Well, that's a risk I'm willing to take. How 'bout you, Avery?" Mel makes a sound of agreement, and grins as she comes to a stop light. "Avery says, 'suck it.' She's not taking a charity case either. Go ahead. Sic your big thug on us. I'll cut him up and don't you doubt that I won't. Yeah." She nods for a few seconds and then a smile breaks across her face like sunlight in the dawning sky. "Damn straight, woman. That's more like it. We'll be there in an hour. We both need wardrobe, too." Mel tosses me back the phone.

I'm a little afraid. I put it to my ear like it might bite me, but Black already hung up. "Are you insane? She threatens to beat the shit out of us and you said bring it?"

Mel shrugs. "It's part of the game, honey. If you can't play, get out of the sandbox." I blink at her like she's lost her mind. Mel rolls her eyes, "This business is just that—a business. If Black wants to work us like this, then she's gotta compensate us. That's all there is to it."

"Has she ever had Gabe or one of the guys rough you up?"

Mel snorts and glances at me. We turn a corner and head back to the Long Island Expressway. "Where are you getting your info on pimping? *Crocodile Dundee?* This isn't 1980, Avery. The most Black will do is make you uncomfortable."

"You don't believe that."

"It's all talk. Have you ever seen Gabe beat the shit out of anyone?"

"Yeah. Last week. He beat Henry Thomas—"

"So he slapped him around in front of you, but did you witness the whole asskicking?"

"No."

"Well, I've never seen one either. Odds are that Mr. Dickhead is walking around in the same condition you last saw him in— meaning that Gabe threw a few punches and that was it. If it's bend over or take a hit, I'd rather get punched in the face. Besides, Black was bluffing this time. She needs us."

"Yeah, but the key phrase is *this time*, Mel." What about next time? Or the time after? What happens when we no longer hold the same value to Black? I don't want to find out.

CHAPTER 5

The life of a call girl agrees with Mel. She likes to make guys fall on their knees. She tells me that Black gives her the guys that want to be tamed, that need a strong woman. "Most women are too demur. Bunch of pussies." We're sitting in the office, checking in.

I stifle a laugh because Black is coming back. She already scolded me for being fat again, even though my measurements are exactly the same. "Avery," Black snaps her fingers at me, motioning to take the lingerie in her hands, "Put these on and hurry up. You're going to be late."

"She's not late and stop snapping at her like she's a mutt. Show some respect." Mel folds her arms over her chest. She's leaning back in a chair, already dressed and ready to go.

"Why are you still here?" Black's eyes narrow to slits as she stares at Mel.

"I'm waiting for my friend."

"Your friend has had enough of you for today. Go and have the driver take you downtown before I get tired of seeing you." Black glares at Mel and Mel stares back. They hate each other. It's weird, since I thought they had an okay relationship. Guess not.

Mel backs down first, which is weird. She stands and brushes her dress off. "Fine, but if you mess with her—"

"Yes, you'll personally carve me a new face. I understand your gang speak. Now go on." Black uses the most condescending tone I've ever heard. I can't believe Mel doesn't say anything back, but she doesn't.

Instead, there's a languid smirk on her face that clearly accompanies the word, BITCH.

Black turns back to me and doesn't notice, or care. "Well, hurry up!"

I dress quickly and pull on the bra and panty set. Another shelf bra. The underwire cuts into my sides because it's a size too small. My boobs look like popovers in this thing, which isn't a look I usually go for. It's not the 60's, no one likes cone-shaped boobs anymore. I walk out and Black hands me a little charcoal gray dress. "Uh, Miss Black, this doesn't fit."

Her eyes flick up from her desk and she looks me over. "It's fine. This client will enjoy it. Get the dress on and get out of here."

Gabe is waiting for me downstairs. The ground looks like a sheet of glass. It's been raining, which makes the city lights sparkle on the ground. I love the city when it rains, especially since I don't have to try and catch a cab. I duck into the car and lose a boob as I climb in. It falls out of the too-small bra and peeps out the top of my low-cut neckline. Horrified, I tuck it back into the bra as Gabe walks around the car and lets himself in. He doesn't say anything.

We drive to another hotel, to meet another client. My stomach is twisting ruthlessly as I cross the lobby. It isn't until I lift my hand to knock on the door that I realize that I never saw this guy's picture or caught his name. All the bickering between Black and Mel had me distracted. Just as I raise my fist to knock, the door opens and a hotel employee greets me.

"Good evening, Miss. Your husband said he'd be along shortly and asked me to make some preparations to your room. I hope everything is to your liking. There's a letter on the desk, from Mr. Charles. He asked that you read it immediately and apologized for his delay." The young man holds the door open for me and I step inside.

For a second my heart is pounding, but when I glance around the room there are roses everywhere. Some of the jitters float away as I stand there. Then it dawns on me to tip the guy. I stuff twenty bucks into his palm and thank him.

When he leaves, it's clear that I'm alone. "Well, let's see where Mr. Charles has gone to..." I can't believe he made a fuss about me being here and then didn't show up. I still get paid, so whatever.

After finding the letter, I tear it open and read the note. I stare at it for a second longer than I should, not believing what I'm reading. *It can't be…*

My phone chirps and I drop the letter. Grabbing my purse, I yank out my phone and look down at the screen. It's Sean. A smile softly laces across my face.

There's a text message.

Avery, are you there?

Yes, I type back with a stupid smile on my face. He really booked me again? Maybe he doesn't want to let me go and just can't say it yet. I cradle the phone to my chest like it's Sean and giggle.

Do you understand what I want us to do? He explained it in his letter. Since he can't be here, Sean wants to be dirty with me from afar.

Heart pounding, I type back, *Sexting, right?*

Pretty much. I couldn't be there, but I had to have you.

Miss Black will have a coronary if she finds out about this. Pictures are discouraged and sexting is strictly forbidden. But it's Sean... I start to ask him if he cleared it with Black, but erase the message. I want to be with him and if he didn't, I'd rather not know. As it is, I wonder what Gabe will report since he isn't going to see Sean walk in or out.

I'm not sure what to do, or what to type. How do we even start something like this? I flat out tell him, *I haven't done this before...*

A few seconds pass and he writes back, *It's okay. I'll tell you what to do and you do it. That's all. It's not hard, Avery... Stand in front of the mirror and take a picture of yourself. I want to see what you're wearing.*

I walk to the mirror and click the picture. After I hit send, another message appears.

Remove the dress and send another...

My heart flutters. This is weird. There's no one to talk to, no one to look at, but I do it anyway. This is what he wants. Besides,

I've never done it before. Maybe it's not going to be weird the whole time. Slipping the dress off my shoulders, I take another picture showcasing my cleavage and perky nipples, but it doesn't feel sexy. I'm too nervous. I click send and glance around the room.

There's wine on the dresser. It's the kind you like. Go have a glass and then lay down on the bed.

Fine by me. I walk across the room in my heels and find the wine. Someone already removed the cork so the only thing I have to do is pour a glass and chug it. The wine warms me as it floods my stomach. That combined with a lack of dinner makes me calm down. I pour another glass and place it on the nightstand before climbing onto the bed.

There's another message:

Are you ready?

Yes.

Will you do anything I want, no questions asked?

My stomach twists as giddy excitement rises in my chest. *Yes, if that's what you want...*

Good. Tonight is about me seeing you. I'll tell you what to do and when. I want you to follow my directions exactly and send pictures or video when I tell you.

Will you send any to me?

No. Tonight's about your ecstasy, Avery. I want to see you writhing with pleasure and know that I was the man who did it to you...that my words were enough to make you come hard and long. The message makes my stomach flip. The spot between my legs is already pulsing softly, expectantly. The whole situation is unreal. I thought Sean left me. I thought we'd never see each other again, and here we are.

I have a little buzz from the wine and intend to keep it that way, so I take another swig, downing half the glass. I'm nervous. I'm a sexting virgin and don't want to do it wrong, but at the same time, this scares the life out of me. A lazy smile forms on my face as the wine takes effect.

Sean tells me to do things, things that normally make me blush. Before I have time to think about it, my hand is down my panties and between my legs. Using my other hand, I send him a picture like he asked.

A few seconds later, there's another message, *Damn, that's hot. Rub your clit with your thumb and slip your finger into your pussy for me, baby.*

I'm not ready yet… Although I feel my body reacting to his words, I'm not quite there yet. I expect him to say something else when he responds, but he doesn't redirect my hands.

No hesitating, Avery. Do it. I take a breath, do as he says, and force my finger inside. *What does it feel like?*

Hot…tight.

Good. Rub your thumb over your clit, and push in deeper, as hard as you can.

I do as he says and my fingers grow slick. He has me do it three times in a row, snapping a picture of my face and another of my hand disappearing into my panties. I don't look at the pictures, because I'll lose my nerve. Instead, I just give him what he wants and try to stop thinking about what I'm actually doing. So far none of the pictures are horribly incriminating, but they get that way pretty fast.

As soon as I'm hot and bothered, Sean has me strip and send him naked pictures of me pinching my nipples and then more with my hand between my legs. For a while the texts tell me to keep massaging myself, so I do. It's so different, so erotic. I've never done anything like this and it just feels so dirty. All the pictures, the filthy texts, and the way he commands me—it makes me incredibly hot. I want him to touch me so badly, but he's not here. I follow his commands and work my hand, pushing my finger in and out in slow deep motions. Warm coils of lust snake around my hips, making my insides tighten. God, I wish he was here, touching me, doing this to me with his hands and his mouth. Moaning, I close my eyes for a second and sigh.

The phone chirps and I look at the screen. *Show me.*

A chill runs through me. I know what he means, but that picture crosses a line in my mind. I hesitate, not wanting to take a picture of that part of me—doing that with my fingers. It's so sexual, so graphic. My heart pounds harder as I think about it.

Another message appears, *Avery, I want you to show me. Put the phone between your legs and take the picture. I want to see that your fingers are where I want them. Come on, baby… be the slutty, sensual woman I know you are. Show me your fingers in your pussy, baby.*

I'm gasping for air as my heart pounds faster. I can't do that… but I want to. For him, I want to. Stop thinking! Sean said that over and over when he was here, but he hasn't said it tonight. I want to be everything he could possibly want. I feel slutty, and I feel like doing it, but something inside my mind is screaming not to. But I want to… I want to cross that line, I want to show him that I'll do anything he asks me to. There's something about having him command me that takes my breath away. I want him to own me, to have me any way he wants. I lower the phone and take the picture, pressing send before I have a chance to chicken out. My fingers continue to massage my slick skin, and it's getting harder to maintain the slow teasing pace. I feel my body growing hotter and more insistent, as it grabs my finger harder and tighter each time I slip out.

His message puts a smile on my face, *Oh fuck, that's sexy, baby. But that one finger isn't enough. Add the other three and push in hard. Do it. Show me. I'm so hard for you right now, Avery. I wish I could bend you over and fuck you all night. Show me baby…*

My body is so off kilter. I want the release, but one finger isn't really getting me anywhere and the way he has my thumb just teases me. Slipping in two more fingers inside isn't hard, but when I try to add the fourth, it's tight.

Not sure if I can…

Don't stop, baby. Rock your hips into your hand over and over again. Push deeper every time. Do it.

I try to do what he says, and rock my hips, pushing my hand in deeper and deeper. Raw sounds of sexual pleasure are pouring from my throat. I'm so slick and it feels so good. Add to the fact that the whole thing is so wrong and I'm euphoric. There's something so dirty about this, so carnal that lust is making my body feel things I haven't felt before. My hair tangles around my face as I writhe on the bed, bucking my hips into my hand. All four fingers are inside, stretching me, pushing deeper and making me cry out. My nipples are hard, and ache, wanting to be touched. I wish Sean was here to suck on them, to taste my breasts and tease me into oblivion.

The phone chirps. *I want to see you lose it. I want to watch you shove your fist into your tight, wet pussy and see the look on your face when you come. There's a piece of Velcro in the drawer and another on the ceiling. Switch to video for me baby. My dick is so hard. I've been stroking it in my hand, rubbing, imagining you on your knees in front of me. If you could swallow my cock right now… Avery, baby, put me out of my misery. Let me watch you come…*

His words shoot through my body, igniting a wave a lust. *Anything for you…*

My legs wobble as I stand on the bed, and attach the phone to the ceiling. I fall onto my back and say to the camera, "I miss you, baby," and then my mouth starts uttering phrases I'd never say to anyone. I talk about his dick and all the things I'd like to do with it as I pump my hand deeper into my slick core. Carnal sounds come from my throat as the burning coils of lust tighten inside me.

I fight it, I don't want to come yet, but my hand doesn't stop. All four fingers push in deeper, harder as my other hand tugs my nipples. My thumb rubs against my clit teasing me, making me completely out of control. My mouth opens as I gasp for air like I can't breathe. I don't think about how I look or what he'll do with this video when it's over. I don't think at all. I act like the animal he wants me to be, hot and wet, purring with desire and continue to beg for his dick any way that he'll give it to me. I beg him to fuck my face and pull my hair until he comes in my mouth. I start to think about that as my fingers thrust into me harder and faster, and I can feel the beautiful ripples begin. Lust pulls me higher, until I can't stand it another second. I need the release. My control shatters and the pulsing begins, making me drive my hand in harder and faster.

I scream out his name as I come in front of him, hips bucking wildly, pushing harder and deeper with each thrust. I shatter brilliantly, with ecstasy on my face and my back arched off the bed with my hand nearly all the way inside of me. I hold my body rigid as the delicious pulsing overtakes me, gasping for air between wild pleas.

By the time I still, my heart has slowed. I glance up at the phone with heavy eyelids and grab it. Pulling it to my lips, I kiss the screen and say, "I love you, baby."

After sending the video, I lay back on the bed with a sated smile on my face. It's quiet for a little bit before the texts start again.

Holy fuck, that was hot. Next time I see you, you can bet my dick is going straight into that dirty mouth of yours. I mean, Avery... Wow.

I smile and type back, *Did you come?*

Fuck, yeah. I'm lucky I didn't get the phone wet. Damn, Avery. That was beyond sexy...

I roll onto my stomach and type, *What now?*

We do it again. I have a few more positions for you to try and a lot of Velcro.

CHAPTER 6

I can't wipe the stupid smile off my face as I slip into my room early the next morning. There's no sign of Naked Guy. Bonus!

A squeal has been building in my throat, but I keep swallowing it back. I'm really doing it. I'm going to see Sean and I'm going to ask him to marry me. The thought of actually doing it makes me feel so queasy, but it's a good kind of sick—like Christmas Eve, can't-wait-for-Santa kind of sick.

As I shove a pair of socks into my bag, Amber strolls out of the shower with a towel on her head and another barely covering her boobs. Why did I get the exhibitionist roommate? Part of me thinks if the woman dropped her towel that she'd continue to prance around the room like I think she's hot. Maybe Amber's a nympho and doesn't know it. Or maybe she does and I don't. Whatever. I'm just glad to get out of here for the night.

Amber crosses the room to her closet. Clothes stick out from her drawers and everything is wrinkled. She picks out something and pulls it on, not caring if my back is turned. "So," she says as she lights up a cigarette. "Where are you off to on this insanely warm Sunday morning? Visiting the dead parents? The dead sea serpents? Or the nasty-ass, but totally fuckable, scary guy?" She lets out a stream of smoke and sits at the window, looking out into the square below.

I glance over at her. "Scary guy."

"Ah, so he did get to you?"

I'm not sure what she means. "Yeah, I guess so."

Amber nods and continues enjoying her cigarette like it's something phallic. The way her lips wrap around it and slip over the tip as she goes to exhale is disturbing. "So the bad boy rocked your socks off and you're blowing off school a few weeks before finals to have a fun day, is that it? I guess you're over that good girl act, now."

"It wasn't an act."

Amber laughs. "Yeah right. With the way you've been putting out, I think we should both stop pretending and just call the sheep black."

"What the hell are you smoking over there? You make no sense at all. I'm not sleeping around—"

Amber laughs like a man and rolls her eyes. "Whatever, bitch. We both know you're lying. Tell yourself anything you want so you can look in the mirror in the morning, but we both know how you're spending your nights."

Turning my head, I look over my shoulder—pausing with a shirt in hand, above my bag—and glare at her. I wonder if she knows about my employment, but that's not possible. A cold feeling snakes down my throat and coils in my stomach. Amber doesn't elaborate, which makes me think she's just messing with my head.

I change the subject. "So, where's Naked Guy? Off fucking some other dorm today?"

"Ha ha. He's coming by later to show me his anal beads collection and I—"

Oh my God! Spinning on my heel, I snap at her, "TMI! Keep your fucking preferences to yourself. It's bad enough I know what his thingie looks like. I don't need—"

"His *thingie?*" she mocks. "What's the matter, Avery? Can't say the real word?" Amber's eyes glitter. She honed in on my little word and is advancing across the room, cigarette still in hand. "Is it just too much to wrap your little mouth around? Cock, dick, penis? Pick one and say it." She stops in front of me, looking down at me like I'm a child. One arm is across her chest and the other is holding the burning smoke off to the side. She tilts her head, watching me. "Go on—say it."

I smile tritely, but she's unnerving me. The way she looks at me is so smug, with a dash of hostility. Most mornings she spends trying to stay in bed, because she stayed up fucking all night. I glare at her. "I'm not reciting male genitalia for you."

She laughs lightly and says it again, whispering the word in a creepy way, close to my face. "I bet you scream when you come and say all sorts of dirty shit. It's the good girls that have the kinkiest stuff going on in their heads." Amber looks down into my bag and pulls up one of my G-strings. She holds it on her pointer finger and raises a brow at me. "See what I mean?"

I snatch it back from her and shove it into my bag. "At least I wear panties."

"Ouch." Amber feigns offense and then snorts and turns away shaking her head. "Me and you could have a lot of fun. Roommates who do three-ways never sleep alone."

I make a face and look over at her. "If you ever suggest that again, I'll puke all over you."

"Whatever. Go on and pretend to be a nun. I don't care."

"Nuns don't sleep with guys."

She grins, "Well, not all at once, anyway. Maybe I should join a convent." She taps her front tooth with her finger like she's thinking about it.

I know what she's thinking. "Nuns don't do confession. Priests are the only ones who get to use the box, so think of something else or have someone stab you with a cross. Maybe you'll turn back into a werewolf and can go hump a tree for the rest of the day."

She gives me a snotty look and sticks her tongue out. "Bitch."

"Whore."

"Slut."

"Skank."

"Hooker." Amber says the word exactly the same way she said the others, but she's acting so weird today. I lift my chin slightly before throwing another insult her way. Amber is watching, waiting for me to show any sign of weakness. Does she know? Is that what this is about? Did she find out that I'm working for Black? That would suck. She'd tell Black that I'm in love with Sean.

I don't pause. "Hoe," I throw back, but our eyes hold a second too long.

"Bitch."

"You already said that one." I zip my bag shut and throw it over my shoulder.

"Yeah, but it suits you—a bitch in heat. Am I right?"

"Yeah, okay... I'm only going to say this once. If you have something to say to me, say it to my face, now. I'm not doing this weird shit with you when I get back, so if you've got something you want to say to me, spit it out."

Amber purses her lips and then smiles at me, before rolling back onto her bed. "As if I'd make your life so simple. Catch you later, cock-lover. Make sure you ask him to get your back door really good and hard. You're in serious need of an alignment. No one should be this bitchy right after sex." She raises a brow at me and laughs.

I roll my eyes and walk out to the sound of her hollow laughter bouncing off the walls.

CHAPTER 7

Before I get to my car, Mel comes chasing after me. "That was some crazy shit last night. What'd your guy want?" She practically yells as she runs at me and crosses the parking lot. "Where you goin'?"

"To see Sean, and shut up. That was way too loud and I think Amber knows." I glance around to make sure she didn't follow us into the parking lot.

Mel waves me off. "Amber doesn't know shit."

"Mel, she knows. I don't know how, but she does. She's trying to get me to do three-ways with her and say 'cock.' Two days ago she would have never suggested such a thing." I reach for my trunk, open it, and toss in the bag. When I slam it, the lid bounces back up and nearly smacks me in the face. "Awh, damn it!" I slam it down again and it catches this time.

"Amber is just trying to get dirt on you. She probably has some dick that only wants a three-way, and the only person she can offer up is you. You better be ready for her to have some asshole in your room one night, and hope you trip on them coming in the door. By the way, if you do, that doesn't count as a threesome."

"What the hell is it with people and three ways?" I stare at her. Mel sounds like she's had a few and thinks they're good, like chicken soup.

"You don't see the appeal? Come on, you have to see it. Two dicks at once..." She gets a funny look on her face, like she's remembering something.

I look away like I haven't noticed. "Fine, maybe, but two girls for one guy is a dude fantasy. I see enough of naked Amber without having sex with her." I cringe and shake it off, but the mental image is stuck. "Oh gross, I'm gonna have to bleach my brain after this conversation."

Mel laughs. "Clorox hasn't made brain bleach, yet. Otherwise I'd have a stockpile for you, because have I got stories for you!"

"Mel, I don't have time. I have a ring." Taking a deep breath, I smile at her. "I'm going to find Sean and ask him to marry me."

"No shit? I thought that was all talk. Even after work last night? You sure about this?"

"Work last night was Sean—"

She blinks and leans in like she didn't hear me. "Come again? I thought Ferro left town."

"He did, but we, ah… did it anyway." I give her an awkward smile and hope to God she catches on.

Mel glances both ways and says in a low voice, "You had phone sex?"

"Sorta. Maybe…"

She shakes her head at the same time her jaw drops open. "You did not sext with him. Black will fire your ass faster than a—"

"It's what he wanted. Besides, it's Sean."

"She won't care, Avery. Damn, you know the rules. What the hell were you thinking?" She glances up at me. "I'm going with you and we're taking my car."

"Yeah, I don't think so."

"And you think I'm letting you go by yourself? Besides, I need to slap that boy in the head. Rules are rules. They're there for a reason. You know what happens to us if we get caught, right? Those pictures are proof. There's not supposed to be any proof of anything."

"Sean isn't going to report us to the cops. Besides, if he did, he'd get in trouble, too. If you stop lecturing me and can be ready to go in five minutes, I'll wait for you. If Amber happens on me, I'm running her over." I shiver. Holy crap she creeped me out.

"Fine, but I'm not done bitching you out yet. How long's the ride to Jersey?"

"A few hours."

"Good, that should be long enough to drive into your head how stupid that was, and then you can give me details." Mel rubs her hands together, grins, and runs back to the dorm.

———

Mel is in the passenger seat in my car. It runs okay and gets great gas mileage, but the rickety nature of the rusted frame makes Mel jumpy. Plus we have to yell because the window seals are pretty much shot.

"So, I wanna see some pictures of the infamous Sean Ferro in compromising positions… or at least his naked ass." She holds out her hand for my phone.

"Uh, it wasn't like that."

She stares at me for a second. "He didn't send you any pictures at all?"

"No. Why? Is that weird?"

Mel makes a face and picks up my phone. "Depends on what he said. May I?" She holds up my phone and I know she wants to look at the messages.

My face flames red, but I nod anyway. "Since when do you ask?"

"Since when do I go through your personal shit? Never, that's since when. I might butt my nose where it don't go, but I—" Her eyes go big as she reads the screen. "He had you do this shit? Like all of it?" Her eyes continue to read as I answer.

"Yeah…" I'm getting the impression that something is off. "I've never done it before."

"No shit."

"So, did I do it wrong?"

"I don't know. To each his own, you know, but it's weird he didn't send you some dick shots or something—maybe even record himself jerking off so you can see." She squints at the screen and turns it sideways like there's a hidden dick in the letters.

"It sounded like he wanted to do that another time."

She puts the phone down and looks over at me. "I didn't picture him as the type. Shows what little I know." She shrugs. "So, little Miss Chastity Belt, did that get you off? I'm not watching the video. By the way, you should delete that shit. If you lose your phone, it'll be on YouTube faster than you can say fuck me."

"I know. I'll delete it. I don't like having stuff like that around, at the same time, it was with Sean." I smile into space.

"You look like you've been hit in the head with a brick, Avery. Stop that. Sean is trouble. Like a big fat sack of damaged goods. Marrying him means you're okay with all his shit—the hookers, his dead wife, and his freaky ass family. Did you think this through?" Mel moves her hand to recline her seat. Before I can stop her, she pulls the lever and the seat falls back. She spews some choice words as she flies backwards. "What the fuck?"

"Steve's broken—uh, the seat." I reach for the chair back, but I can't help her fix it since I'm driving. Mel gives me a look, so I explain, "Yeah, I named him Steve the Seat. He does all the way up or all the way down. That chair isn't really into foreplay—no in the middle. He's an all or nothing kind of chair."

She laughs and spews spittle all over the dashboard. "Oh my God. You've been hanging out with me way too long! You've turned your passenger seat into a personified pervert."

"Steve thanks you for sitting on him. He hasn't had this much action since Sean used a screwdriver on his little bits. Steve likes things rough." Grinning, I look out the windshield and change lanes to take the Tunnel.

Mel cracks up and before too long we're on the Turnpike, headed straight for Cherry Hill. Peter gave me the information last time I saw him. It's weird, but I like Sean's family. Normally, I feel like I don't fit in—like at all—but Peter was easy to talk to. I didn't feel like he was looking down at me, even though he knows what I do. Gotta admit, that's weird—and awesome. Especially since he didn't proposition me later.

Mel chatters about nothing for a long time, keeping my mind off of Sean, but whenever a lull works its way into the conversation, there he is—Sean Ferro. Mel's question prompted another one in my mind. It's not that I can't accept Sean's past, it's more a question of whether or not I can handle what it means for the future. Will his dark side get darker? Will Sean still need the different faces of nameless women to control to forget what he lost? Sean said he doesn't want that anymore, but what if that need comes back? What happens when I'm not enough? I don't expect to overshadow his past, and there's no way to just walk away and forget about it. If that were true, neither of us would be hanging out in graveyards, talking to the dead.

Can I handle Sean day in and out? Do I want to? A guy like Marty—a normal guy, with normal problems—would give me a normal life. Isn't that what I wanted— normal—as in a little Cape Cod with pansies on the porch and kids under foot? Sean isn't that guy, so it washes that future away and I can't picture what my life will be or who will be in it with that footing removed.

How do you pull someone out of hell anyway? Is it even possible? Growing up, I'd heard to never reach out. If a person slips off a ledge, the only way to help them is to throw down a rope or something. If you reach out, they pull you down with them. I'm terrified that I'm reaching out, that there's no rope, and it'll destroy us both. Maybe Sean knows that. Maybe that's why he left.

But he wants you. He sexted with you. Sean wouldn't have done that if we were making a clean break, would he?

I feel the wedding band I picked out for him in the pocket of my jeans. I guess it's more of an engagement ring than a wedding band. I wanted something different, and I found it. The ring is white gold with a Celtic pattern carved into the band. A single blood red stone is woven into the pattern and sits on the top of the ring. It's exactly what I wanted, Old World looking, but still a band—a circle—the symbol that means eternity.

Mel tries to put Steve back into an erect position, and comments on it. "Dude has issues getting a boner, doesn't he?"

I laugh. "Yeah, you gotta rub him just right or he doesn't stay up."

"We're both going straight to Hell. You know that, right? Damn, we're sick. Sick, I tell you!" She's laughing, trying to get the seatback to stay up, but Steve isn't feeling it. "Well, now what?"

"Rub him harder?"

Mel bursts out laughing. "You're so fucked up. You know that right? I think you had this mentality for messed up shit before I brought you to Black. As much as I regret that, it's nice to see you acting out on your… uh, whatever the hell is wrong with you."

"Oh, shut up. There's duct tape in the glove box. Tape him up."

Mel gives me a weird look and then does it. She runs a piece of tape behind her chair, after pulling it up and ties it around mine and her door. She leans back gingerly, expecting to topple over, but it holds. "Viagra for the challenged chair." She holds up the duct tape and nods, before stuffing it back in the glove box. "So, how do we find him?"

"Peter said Sean's been around. I guess we go into stalker mode and play 'spot the biker' until we find Sean."

"You don't have an address?"

"It's not like it's the City," by which I mean Manhattan. "Besides, if that doesn't work, we can try hotels. There are only a few here and I doubt they're all having biker conventions this weekend."

"Fine, but you gotta buy me some pancakes when we're done here. I feel the need to spread the urban legend of the IHOP blow job into the TriState Area." She smirks at me and nods, while tucking her hands behind her head like she's too awesome for words. The movement makes the tape slip and her seat falls back.

I nearly crash the car because I'm laughing so hard. Tears sting my eyes by the time we take the exit, and it's strange to be laughing so hard when I'm about to do something that scares me to death. My emotions never respond the right way at the right time, but I'll take any laughter when and where I can get it. Life's been too damn hard lately and a fit of giggles is good for the soul.

CHAPTER 8

We pull off the road and fix Mel's seat so that she isn't duct taped to the door anymore. When Steve fell over, all the tape went down too. Some of it sprung back and stuck to her hair. Talk about words I thought I'd never hear. Mel gave me an earful and threatened to castrate the seat (although I'm not sure if that's possible).

"Avery, this isn't going to work." Mel groans. Half a second later, she cocks her head like a terrier. "Well, I'll be damned.

There it is." Mel holds up a finger and points at the shiny bike Sean bought with me on Long Island. It's parked out back at a hotel, right next to the back door.

I hesitate. "Should I go in and look for him?"

"They probably won't give you his room number, but I could get it for you. What do you want to do?"

"Follow him around and see what he's doing. How creepy does that sound?" I glance over at her, knowing it's past creepy, but I'm curious about what was so urgent that he had to run off.

Mel shrugs. "Fine by me, but I need some food. There's a Wag-a-Bag back there. Let's grab something and stalk him the right way."

We load up on carbs and soda and sit across the street. My car isn't really noticeable in a parking lot, but if Sean spots it, he'll know it's me. I mean, how many old Capris are still running around?

I park the car at the convenience store, facing the street, so we can see his bike and sit back to wait. Mel opens a bag of Bugles and puts the cone-shaped chips on her fingertips. "I'll get you and your little dog too, my pretty little call girl." Her voice is a perfect witch's imitation.

"You're not quite green enough to pull that off." I snatch a Bugle from her fingertip and pop it in my mouth.

Shifting back to Mel's normal don't-screw-with-me voice, she sways her head and waves a finger in my face. "Don't you go saying nothing about the color of my skin. I could make a perfectly perfect nasty witch—"

"I know."

"Hey!"

"Mel, you walked right into that one. What's with you lately?" Mel seems distracted. That's the best word for it. It's like she's here, but her mind is somewhere else. Grinning at her, I elbow her side. "So, who is he?" It was a wild stab in the dark, but by the way she turns her claws on me, I know I guessed right.

"What the fuck makes you think there has to be some—" Her hackles are raised and I brace for impact, but at the same second, I see Sean walk out of the hotel across the street.

Lifting my hand, I point. "It's him."

Mel slaps me. "Put that down. If he looks over here, he'll see you wagging your finger at him. Slip down into your seat. I'll see which way he goes and then we can follow."

"He's not going to see me. We're all the way across the street. Besides, look at him—he's totally spaced out." Sean is the kind of guy who usually soaks up the details of everything around him with a flick of his eyes, but today, his gaze is downcast. The warm weather and the sun doesn't melt the frost that's formed on his shoulders, either. Sean looks every bit as dangerous as he did going head to head with Henry. Cringe, that was the worst mistake ever, Henry, I mean.

It's really strange thinking about it, but Henry seemed like a nice guy on the outside. Meanwhile, Sean seems like he's actively looking for a puppy to kick because it would amuse him. All this time I thought the happy-go-lucky people were the ones carrying their hearts on their sleeves, but I don't think that's true anymore. It's the people with that ferocious I'll-eat-you-alive look—the folks that scare the bejesus out of old ladies—those are the people with their heart on their sleeves. The barbs in their vacant stares aren't animosity or hatred, but pain and brokenness. At some point it becomes impossible to hide how many pieces they've shattered into and you get this charred outer shell that's brittle as hell, and impossible to fix.

When I look at Sean, that's what I see. What looks like a bitter, arrogant man is actually just another guy trying to hold it together. Dad used to say that when things got rough, having Mom around was like having a brace. Even if they both tipped to the side, if they leaned toward each other, they wouldn't fall down. Being alone means falling flat on my face.

Sean must sense someone is looking at him, because his gaze lifts and searches the parking lot, his face slowly scanning the people.

"Oh shit!" I squeal and slink down at the same time Mel smashes my head into the dashboard. I yelp, but she doesn't take her hand off the back of my neck. Instead, she sits there, leaning against her door, and looks behind us, like she's waiting for someone to come out of the store.

"And he's still looking…" she says over her shoulder. When her hand releases the back of my neck, I can breathe a little better, but I don't sit up. "What the hell is he doing out here, anyway?"

"Something with his brother, Peter."

"Pete Ferro is here too? Shit, add one more and it could be a Ferro family reunion. I bet they'd all kill each other before we got to dessert." Mel leans her head against her hand after propping her elbow up on the door. "He don't know your license plate number, right?"

"That was so grammatically disgusting. Why do you talk like you took a brick to the head?"

Her foot gently kicks me, originally aimed for my side, but I turned my head and the tip of her sneaker goes into my mouth. Mel yanks her foot back as I spit out gravel, gum, and other parking lot nastiness. "Oh, that was foul. I didn't mean to make you eat shoe. Sorry about that."

I'm spitting and resisting the urge to strangle her. "The laughter kind of negates the apology there, Mel."

"Well, you asked for it. All making fun of my intellectuality. I'm a smart girl. I can handle myself."

"So, why do you flip between talking like an intellectual and a bag lady?"

"You don't understand nothin'. I'm me and I let you see both sides of my life—the good and the bad. They mix together and fall out of my mouth in ubiquitous sentences that I got no control over. You think this mind can be reproduced? Hell no, and it won't be tamed either, so keep your comments on my urban vernacular to yourself, thank you very much."

"You're welcome very much. Not that you make sense or anything, but is he gone? I didn't hear the bike start up and my head hurts from getting slammed into the dashboard. Thanks for that too, by the way."

"Psh, whatever." Mel waves me off. "I'm helping you develop some character. All white girls need a little color here and there."

"Not in the form of bruises. Come on, where is he, Mel?"

She smirks. "Oh, he's gone." Chuckling to herself, Mel continues, "He drove off a few minutes ago and went that way."

I sit up and give her a girlie slap, the kind where hands are a blur of motion and it's more annoying than anything. "You suck! We're going to lose him."

We pull out of the parking lot and follow Sean's bike, leaving several cars between us. "Damn we're conspicuous. The only way we'd be more noticeable was if your horn played La Cucaracha. It doesn't, does it?"

"No." I drop back further and hide behind a truck. Mel tells me where he turned and once we're on side streets, it's much harder to hide. "Where the hell is he going?"

"Beats me if I know." But her voice is tight like she does know and it isn't good. We're in the middle of suburbia, complete with lawns, houses, and families.

"What do you think he's doing over here?"

Mel doesn't answer this time. Instead, she says, "Pull over and let's find out. He stopped a few houses down."

I slip over to the side of the road and park next to a minivan. I can't see much, so I lean over to Mel's side of the car. Mel is tense and it takes me a second to see why. After Sean parks his bike, he walks over to a woman standing on the front lawn of a cute house. A work crew is putting in a white picket fence, beautiful flower-filled gardens, and painting the little home so it looks like new.

The woman matches Sean's height with inky black hair that's tied into a neat chignon at the base of her neck. The dress she's wearing fits her perfectly. The longer I sit and stare, the more I wish I had no eyes. The two of them seem comfortable together, like there's a relationship there. This can't be what it looks like. I slip back into my seat and glance at Mel. "Well, what's he doing?"

The smug smile that's usually lining Mel's lips isn't there. A crease furrows her brow as she stares down the street at the couple and the house. "It could be anything, Avery."

"Yeah, but what's your gut impression?" Mel's quiet for a moment and that's all the answer I need. "Yeah, mine too." I manage to say before swallowing the lump in my throat.

I lean back over to get another look, hoping that it's not what it looks like. Because, to me, it looks like that is Sean's house and this woman is close to him, like in a relationship kind of close. I see it in the way they stand shoulder to shoulder, their bodies turned toward one another. She's not a business associate. His body language is too personal, too intimate for that.

I swallow hard, looking at the white picket fence. That's what I wanted, but it appears that he already has that with someone else. I wonder if the whole family thing was an excuse to take off, to come back here to this woman. But then what the hell was Peter doing? Why'd he come say those things to me. Sean's actually smiling as he leans in close to her ear, closing the space between them. His hand slips around her waist and they stay like that, head to head, talking. Maybe that's not an intimate pose for some people, but it's a step past sex for Sean Ferro. No one is close to him like that. My heart is crumbling in my chest. I wait for them to separate, but they don't.

Mel and I watch them for way too long. The woman touches his hand, arms, and shoulders, pointing and smiling at the house and the yard. Sean doesn't shirk her off like he does with other people. Instead his hand finds the wrist of her hand, and he helps her through the messy yard.

I can't watch any more.

CHAPTER 9

Without a word, I start the car. The engine turns over on the first try. I sit there for a second. Running is for losers. I could get out of the car and stomp down the street like a jaded lover or I could leave and pretend that I never saw any of this—but I did. My stomach is so sour that it feels like I'm going to wretch.

Mel's voice is soft, compassionate. "You want me to walk down there and take his balls off for you, honey?"

I laugh a little and shake my head. "I thought he loved me. How is he making the life I wanted with someone else? He said no to me and yes to her? I don't understand."

"Oh, Avery…" Mel is awkward for a second, like she's thinking about hugging me, but then kicks the door open. "Fuck this. He needs his face rearranged." Before I can stop her, Mel is walking way too fast down the sidewalk.

My eyes go wide and I freeze in place. Before I think, I jump out of the car and race after her. We're in front of a beautiful colonial, two story, home with huge grass plants in the front flowerbeds. As soon as I catch up to Mel, I launch myself at her and we fall into the plants.

"Don't," I beg her, voice shaking as I roll off of her and onto my back.

"Avery," she pushes herself into a sitting position. Blades of grass are stuck in her hair. "He's a douchebag. Telling him so will make—"

"Will make me feel worse. You can't go over there. He has a life with someone else."

"No, I don't." Sean's voice booms behind me. When I look up, he's standing there with the woman two steps behind him, looking irritated beyond belief. Sean is wearing his dark jeans and a tight fitting sweater that makes me want to run my hands over his toned chest. A dusting of stubble lines his cheeks and that dark hair is messy, like he just had sex. "What are you doing here?"

"Looking for you." Mel and I stand and brush ourselves off.

"Did you change your mind?" he asks, and, for a second, Sean looks hopeful.

My eyes glance between him and Mel, and then back to Sean. "Nooo." What? Why does he think that? Confused, I ask, "I thought you missed me?"

Sean looks at the woman standing behind him. "Please, excuse us for a moment." Then he looks at Mel and adds, "Don't rob her while my back is turned."

"Fuck you, Ferro." Mel is tense, ready to fight.

Sean ignores Mel and takes me by my shoulders, trying to pull me away from the group, but I dig my heels in. I'm so confused and mad. How could he do those things with me last night and be like this today? It makes me feel used, so I second guess myself. The thing is, I'm totally sick of doubting everything I do and I won't be handled with kid gloves this time. Screw it.

I muster up a civil tone and manage, "No, say whatever you have to say right here, right now. I'm not doing this with you. You can't say you miss me at night and blow me off during the day."

"Avery, I admit that I'm pleased to see you—a little surprised—but glad all the same. However, I have no idea what you're talking about." He slips his hands into his pockets as a breeze rustles through his hair.

Folding my arms across my chest, I feel the anger about to burst out of my mouth like a geyser. "Of course not. Of course you'd do this. So who is she?" I flip my hand toward the woman watching me like I'm crazy. I probably look insane. I tackled Mel into a plant before Sean walked over. I'm wearing jeans and a ratty sweater with pieces of grass stuck in my hair.

The corners of Sean's lips twitch, as if he wants to smile. "Are you jealous, Miss Smith?"

"Don't call me that, and don't change the subject. Who is she?"

The woman steps forward with a wrinkle at the dead center of her eyebrows. "I think there's been a misunderstanding. I'm Mr. Ferro's assistant for the Granz Project."

"For what now?" Mel barks, folding her arms over her chest. Seriously, Mel and I look like vagrants. All we need is an old shopping cart and a bottle of booze.

"This house. Mr. Ferro is restoring this old home and I'm the person in charge." Her big brown eyes blink at me and then Mel. When no one says anything, she adds, "I'm his employee." A nervous smile flitters across her mouth and then disappears.

Sean continues to stare at me while his business buddy speaks.

Mel clarifies, "So there's no nothing going on between the two of you? You're not his wife, hidden in the suburbs or something?"

The woman's eyes go wide and she takes a step back as her hand covers her heart. "Oh God, no!"

"Yeah, but you seem kinda cozy—"

The woman looks mortified. "I'm a family friend. Sean and I were children together. He gave me this job and that's it. I'm not his wife! I don't even like him." She glances at Sean. "Well, not like that. It'd be like dating my brother." She makes a face and laughs. "Sorry, but that's gross." She pats Sean's shoulder and walks back to the construction in front of the little house.

Sean watches me the entire time, never looking away. Those blue eyes pin me in place, stealing my breath away. Mel slaps me in the back. "Well, then…"

"Yeah…" I say, and rub my hand over the back of my neck, suddenly feeling the need to look at my feet. "So, Granz—isn't that your brother's name?" He nods. "So, you're building him a house?"

"Restoring a house. It's a gift. Did you seriously think that I turned you down because I already had the white picket fence with the wife stashed somewhere?"

Oh God, I can't even look at him. It sounds really bad. He takes my chin in his hand and tips it up. Our gazes lock and my brains fly away. A few stray thoughts bang against my skull like drunk bats. "It seemed reasonable. Nothing else made sense."

He smiles sadly at me. "I told you the truth. I'm not a marrying man. There's too much—" he stops talking and looks over at Mel, who is leaning towards us, not wanting to miss a thing. "Do you mind?"

She puts her hands behind her back and shakes her head. "No, not at all. Go on."

"Ah, Mel…" I ask and smile at her, hoping she'll take a hint and go for a walk.

Mel rolls those amber eyes and then turns on her heel. She chases after the chick working for Sean and asks to see the house. Mel looks over her shoulder at me and points to the front door, telling me that she's going inside. I nod and wave at her.

Turning back to Sean, I don't know what to say. "I've been trying to get on with things and act like you don't matter, but you do. The thing is, I want a relationship with you and there seems to be no way to have one."

Sean leans to the side and drops his helmet to the ground before stepping toward me. His lips are parted like there are things he wants to say, but doesn't know how. The haunted expression that I've seen on his face so many times is lost for the moment. There's no past and no future. All we have is right now and we both know it. We're toe to toe when Sean lifts his hands and brushes his fingers against my cheek. I lean into his palm and hold it to the side of my face as his other hand slips back into my hair. "I know. I've been thinking about you a lot, too."

I smile sadly. "Tell me why. I mean, you mentioned it before, but I felt like you didn't really tell me why you didn't want to get married."

"Avery, don't you see what's standing in front of you? You deserve so much more than I could possibly give you—"

"That's not a reason." I hold onto his hand, but pull it away from my cheek. Keeping his hand in mine, I look at our fingers. They intertwine perfectly. There's no awkward hand holding, where you don't know whose fingers go where, and he doesn't have cactus hands that are covered in calluses. He's perfect for me. He knows it, I feel like he knows it, but he's holding back. I smile grimly and look up at him.

"After last night, I thought we had a shot. I mean, I really thought you might say yes, but I guess I was wrong."

"I don't follow."

I pull the ring from my pocket and place it in his palm. "I bought this for you. I was going to propose."

CHAPTER 10

My voice catches in the back of my throat and I take a deep breath to muffle the sound. Then I smile too brightly and continue to talk, like it's for the best even though I'd rather be shot in the head. "Some things aren't meant to be, I guess. Maybe we're too alike," I shrug and talk to his feet. "I mean, we're both so fucked up that it's amazing we haven't been committed. Getting married would probably just make life harder for both of us. It's not like it'd fix anything, and just because you love someone—well, it doesn't mean anything. Love isn't enough, is it?" I glance up at him and see Sean shake his head.

He looks down at the ring in his palm and turns it over, examining the carved band and the stone. "You picked this out for me?" I nod, like a despondent teenager. If I throw in a 'whatever,' I'd nail it. He lets out a slow rush of air and tilts his head to the side, looking back at me. "Why the pattern and stone? It's an interesting choice for a wedding band."

Tucking a piece of hair behind my ear, I take it back from him and run my finger over the pattern. "It's woven together, string by string, just like life. Sometimes it seems like those little threads snap and we're left hanging. Marriage weaves them together, so even if one string breaks, there are others to hold us up."

"And the stone?"

"Blood binds, but so does pain. I don't know. We've both been through so much that we've bled our hearts out and have nothing to show for it. Maybe that sounds morbid, but that stone looks like a drop of blood. It reminds me of everything we've been through and that we're still standing."

I smile at him shyly and pinch the ring between my thumb and index finger. I hold it up to the sunlight and watch the stone turn bright red. "I was going to ask you to share my life." I take a deep breath and look over at him. Sean's eyes are on the ring, sparkling in the sunlight. His jaw is locked tight, like I said something horrible. I brush his arm with mine and smile at him. "It's fine. I'm not going to ask you."

"You're not?" His eyes flick back to mine.

"No."

"Then, why'd you show me and tell me all that?"

"So you'd know what you are missing."

"Avery," he says, reaching for me. But I step away.

Pocketing the ring, I glance up at him with a soft smile on my face, feeling less fragile than a moment ago. "It's fine. Buy me when you come to town, or do what you did last night, but you have to realize that I'm going to have other clients eventually. Marty can't buy me every weekend."

As soon as Marty's name comes out of my mouth, Sean looks livid. "Marty?"

"Yeah, Marty. I was with him the night before last."

Sean's entire body tenses. He tries so hard to hide it, but he can't. Out of all people to be threatened by—Marty? Seriously? Sean's fingers stretch and bend, as he cracks them one by one. "Anyone else we know?"

Is he jealous? Oh my God, he's sexy when he's like this. I realize that I'm lighting a firecracker with a blowtorch, but I do it anyway. "Henry Thomas. He seems to have an issue with you. Gabe beat the shit out of him when he took it out on me."

That does it. Sean snaps. He steps towards me and pulls me into his arms, crushing me to his chest. It wasn't the reaction I was going for, but I don't protest. His hands grip the back of my head fiercely and when he pulls away he looks a little scary. Okay, very scary. His head twitches ever so slightly as all the muscles in his neck strain so tight that they're ready to pop. "Thomas hurt you?" The words come out one by one. I feel the muscles in his arms flex and relax over and over again, like he's trying to calm himself down but can't.

"A little. It scared me more than hurt me. Why does he hate you?"

Sean presses his eyes closed and pinches the bridge of his nose. "He had something that I wanted a few years back. I took it. He hates me and the feeling is mutual. The only reason I sold him that patent was because of you. I wanted to make you happy, but seeing you with him killed me." Sean looks down at me with a hurricane of emotions in his eyes. "Fuck, and you were with Marty, too? I'm not going to be able to let that guy walk around with his nuts intact, you know that, right?"

"Amber is trying to get me to do a threesome…" I look up into his eyes with my face totally blank. I don't know why I said it—to get a reaction I guess, but Sean just laughs and turns his back on me.

He starts to walk back toward the house. I follow after and fall into step beside him. "Are you?"

"Am I, what?"

"Are you going to do it?" He shakes his head. "Forget it. Don't tell me. You've probably done worse than that for Black, by now." He looks over at me with question in his eyes, like he wants to know, but doesn't.

"I was going to ask you to marry me even though you have some serious issues with sex and call girls. Are you really going to condemn me for being one of those call girls?"

Sean grins at me and shakes his head. "You fucked me in more ways than you will ever know."

"Oh, I think I do."

"No, you seriously don't. I haven't..." his voice drops and he stops. Sean leans in close and rests his hand on my arm. "There's been no one. I can't even tell you how badly I need to feel what that kind of sex makes me feel, but Avery—I can't. You freakin' broke me. I sent a hooker home last night."

"Last night? Wait, what? You were with a hooker last night?"

He nods and looks over at me, rubbing the back of his neck with his hand. "Yeah, well, not for long. I didn't realize it until she got there, but I didn't want her. I wanted you." I blink at him over and over again. He sees the look on my face. "What's wrong?"

"Nothing." Everything. The things he's said that don't make sense start to snap into place. I'm almost too afraid to ask, but I do it anyway. "Uh, Sean. What's your cell number?"

He looks over at me. "Why?"

"Just tell me." He does. The number doesn't match the one in my phone from last night. "Is that your only phone?"

"Yeah..." he's smiling at me, waiting for a punch line that doesn't come. My mind reels, as I realize what's happened. The guy last night, all the messages, the things I typed, the pictures, and videos. Oh God. Horror washes across my face as I stare blankly. I broke every rule Black has, thinking I was doing it with Sean, but it wasn't him. Sean tilts his head to the side and catches my eye. "Avery, what's going on?"

My heart pounds harder, slamming into my ribs. Oh my God. "Someone hired me last night, and pretended to be you."

COMING SOON:

THE ARRANGEMENT VOL 10

*****

THE ARRANGEMENT SERIES

This story unfolds over the course of multiple short novels. Each one follows the continuing story of Avery Stanz and Sean Ferro.

To ensure you don't miss the next installment, text AWESOMEBOOKS to 22828 and you will get an email reminder on release day.

MORE FERRO FAMILY BOOKS

SEAN FERRO
~THE ARRANGEMENT~

******

PETER FERRO GRANZ
~DAMAGED~

******

JONATHAN FERRO
~STRIPPED~

MORE ROMANCE BOOKS BY H.M. WARD

DAMAGED (A Novel)

DAMAGED 2

STRIPPED

SCANDALOUS

SCANDALOUS 2

SECRETS

THE SECRET LIFE OF TRYSTAN SCOTT

And more.

To see a full book list, please visit:

www.SexyAwesomeBooks.com/books.htm

CAN'T WAIT FOR
H.M WARD'S NEXT
STEAMY BOOK?

Let her know by leaving stars and
telling her what you liked about
THE ARRANGEMENT VOL. 9
in a review!

CPSIA information can be obtained
at www.ICGtesting.com
Printed in the USA
LVHW031546141118
597116LV00003B/500

9 780615 859767